Soon I Will

by Claire Daniel

Harcourt

Orlando   Boston   Dallas   Chicago   San Diego

Visit *The Learning Site!*

www.harcourtschool.com

I am an egg.
Soon I will fly.

Some of the eggs hatch.
Soon I will hatch.

Now I am hatched!
I beg for food.

Mama brings us food.
Soon I will get big.

Soon I will fly.
I will fly in the air.

6

I want to fly.
I will fly in the air.

Watch me.
Now I can fly!